LOVE'S REDEMPTION

SWEET AMISH ROMNCE

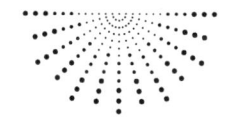

SARAH MILLER

JOIN MY NEWSLETTER

CHAPTER ONE

*Peace I leave with you;
my peace I give you.
I do not give to you as the world gives.
Do not let your hearts be troubled and do not be afraid.
John 14:27*

She couldn't help but wonder if the best parts of her were already gone.

"Come now, Rachel, won't you try?"

Hanna's voice brought Rachel out of her reverie, and she looked up.

"I'm convinced you'll feel much better once you do. A girl needs friends, after all. More after what you've been through than ever before," Rachel Fisher's *ant*, Hanna Fisher, spoke with a solicitous, imploring tone that made Rachel's heart seize with guilt. No matter what kind of pain and loneliness she might be feeling at the moment, it certainly wasn't Hanna's fault, nor Rachel's uncle, Ephraim, either.

Quite the contrary, in fact. Hanna and Ephraim were just about the only thing in the world that mattered to Rachel. Everything else had been ripped away from her, and at the tender age of seventeen, she felt painfully frail and vulnerable.

The sudden passing of her *daed* would likely have destroyed her if it hadn't been for his younger *schweschder*, Hanna, stepping in. However, even now, six months later, she had these dark thoughts. She really couldn't help but wonder if the best parts of her were already gone. Buried in the ground along with her *daed*, lost to her for the remainder of her sorrowful days.

Before the sudden and tragic farm accident had wrenched him away from her, Rachel's *daed* had been her entire world. Her *mamm* had died of a prolonged illness when Rachel was only ten, and after that, her life had practically revolved around the man determined to raise her with all of the love two parents would have given.

Even her looks were taken directly from the man half responsible for giving her life. She had the same golden blonde hair as her *daed*. It had a tendency to grow sandy in the winter months and took on a strawberry hue in the summer. Her eyes were the deep blue of an ocean and always hinted at a wealth of feeling without ever giving away what she was thinking.

She had always loved the fact that she could see her *daed's* eyes looking back at her every time she looked in the mirror, but no more. Now, she could hardly stand to look at her own reflection for the pain it brought her to gaze upon what she saw in her own face.

"*Ach*, please, darling," Hanna said now, reaching for Rachel's hand. "Won't you try and listen to what I'm saying? I know it's hard, and it probably sounds impossibly so, but eventually, it won't feel that way."

The feel of Hanna's warm skin on Rachel's cold, trembling hands was enough to pull her out of her own thoughts, and she did her best to smile in response to words she was only half-listening to. After all the warmth and compassion, Hanna and Ephraim had shown her, the least she could do was try, even if it felt like it might kill her to do so.

"*Jah, Ant* Hanna," she said now, her voice meek and unsure despite her fervent desire to put Hanna's mind at ease. "I hear what you're saying, and I understand. You're right. I know you are, it's just been... hard."

"Of course, it has, darling girl," Hanna cried, pulling Rachel in for a hug that was so fierce Rachel thought it was a wonder that she didn't hear her own ribs cracking. "My *bruder* was a *wunderbaar daed* and a good man. I miss him, too."

"Then how do you do it?" Rachel asked, her voice thick as she pleaded for some light in the darkness. "How do you go on, while all the time, the hole in your heart gets a little bit larger with every passing day?"

"I do it because I know it's what he would have wanted," Hanna answered without a moment's hesitation. "He was so full of life, your *daed*, and the last thing he would want for any of the people he loved is for them to waste away with sorrow over his passing. He's gone to be with *Gott*, Rachel. He's taken care of, and he would want us to go on living our best lives until it's time for us to join *Gott* as well."

Rachel nodded with a little frown, letting Hanna's words wash over her. She'd heard it before, of course, or some variation of what her *ant* was telling her now. Bishop Amos Beiler had said the very same thing when Rachel first arrived in Faith's Creek from Ohio.

Some part of her understood that it was true, just as she knew that Hanna was doing her very best to help her through the darkness. Her *daed* had always been a happy man, full of life, and had sincerely wished everyone around him to find a way to be the same.

"You're right," she said softly now, one of her hands

fluttering to her *kapp* to make sure it was still in place, although she already knew that it was. "He would want me to find a way to be happy."

"That's right," Hanna said eagerly, likely sensing a crack in the wall Rachel had spent the last six months building up and seeking to press her advantage. "And perhaps today would be a good time to give it a try."

"Today?" Rachel asked reticently, already beginning to regret entertaining Hanna's ideas. "What do you mean?"

"After services," Hanna answered with a confident smile. "I know that the young people of Faith's Creek would dearly love to truly make your acquaintance, and perhaps to become real friends. They've respected the space you seemed to need, but that doesn't mean that they won't welcome the chance to really bring you into the community."

"All right, *jah*," Rachel finally said, softly, and more to her folded hands than to Hanna's hopeful face. "I'll do my best. After the services, I'll try and make some friends so that I may carve out a real home for myself in Faith's Creek."

Rachel meant what she said to Hanna, she really did. She reminded herself of that fact as she hurried out of services at their conclusion. She had all but made a promise to her worried *ant* that she would try to put her grieving aside enough that she might be able to join the land of the living instead of letting her heart remain consumed with the dead.

She had fully intended to do what she said, and yet she found herself hurrying away from the other attendees of the services. Just as she had done every time before, she kept her head down and her eyes trained on the ground. She acted as though she were the only person in the world.

If anyone tried to get her attention, she did not see it. If they intended to extend a hand of friendship as Hanna had promised they were so eager to do, she remained oblivious. Promises offered or not; she could not make herself stop.

"I'm all right," she gasped, hurrying away from the people still standing outside of the services. "I just need a moment. I just need to... catch my breath."

She nodded to herself and swallowed hard, an easy task which she nevertheless found painfully difficult. It felt like she was being held within the vice grips of some unseen being, a pressure that would not be lifted until she was completely, blessedly alone.

With this in mind, Rachel moved steadily onward, not allowing herself to slow until she was deep enough in the woods that she didn't think anyone would notice her or follow. Then, with her back to a tree, she let out a sob and slid down to the forest floor.

"I can't, Hanna," she cried miserably, burying her face in her hands. "I know what you want from me, but I simply can't give it!"

That first sob was the one that broke the dam of Rachel's emotions, and for the first time in a long while, she allowed herself to cry. They were big, wild cries that shook her entire body and made her feel as though she would break in two. Part of her hoped that she would. At least that way, she would be free to stop pretending she might somewhere find a place where she fit.

She might have gone right on crying until night fell,

and the countryside descended into darkness without ever noticing. Her pain would have allowed her to forget time, space, and the responsibility she bore to Hanna and Ephraim.

She could have remained rooted to the spot where she fell if it hadn't been for the sound of footsteps coming towards her. When she heard the sound of a twig snapping beneath a boot, however, she looked up sharply, her heart hammering and her eyes widening with fear.

"Who is it?" she demanded, wishing that she sounded more indignant than afraid. "Who's there?"

CHAPTER TWO

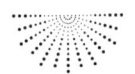

∽

*This is what the L*ORD *says:*
"Restrain your voice from weeping
and your eyes from tears,
for your work will be rewarded,"
*declares the L*ORD.
"They will return from the land of the enemy.
Jeremiah 31:16

∽

Rachel took a deep breath and held it as the sound of someone approaching grew louder. She had the crazy idea that it was *Ant* Hanna come to find her, knowing without having to ask that Rachel could not make the friends she had promised to find.

"Hello?" she called out when she could stand the suspense *nee* longer. "Is there somebody there? Hanna, is that you?"

Her voice was thick with feeling and wavered dangerously, making it all too obvious how close she was to a fresh bout of tears. She got to her feet, and her legs were trembling just as badly as her voice was. Despite going to services with the best intentions in her heart, she had turned the whole endeavor into a dismal failure, and she felt raw and unprepared to meet whoever was coming.

"Hello?" she called again, starting to sound dangerously close to panic now. "Is there somebody out there? Please, show yourself!"

There was still *nee* answer spoken out loud, but the sound of rustling grew louder, and moments later, a figure appeared through the trees. He stopped short when he saw her, and Rachel thought that he looked almost as surprised as she felt. If he had heard her calling, he surely hadn't thought that the words were meant for him.

"*Ach!*" she exclaimed, trying to take a step backward and hitting her back against a tree for her troubles. "I... I'm sorry. I didn't expect it to be you."

It was a ridiculous thing to say, of course, and it only made her feel more foolish than ever. This was precisely why she didn't try to make friends in her new town or at least one of the reasons. Back home, everyone had known her since she was a *boppli*. It made the fact that she was shy, almost obsolete.

Here, in a new place, that was *nee* longer true. She felt that fact more keenly now than she ever had before, alone in the woods with a strange man. If she had seen him before, she couldn't recall it, and she was painfully aware of just how isolated they were now.

There was something about this man that struck her as dangerous, too, although she couldn't exactly say why. Maybe it was because he was at least a head taller than her, for one thing, and broad in the shoulders as well. Despite looking only a handful of years older than her, he had the muscularity of a man who had been working hard for years.

More than anything, though, it was his eyes that made her so nervous. They were such a vivid blue that they almost appeared to be made of ice, and there was something about them that struck her as dangerous. Those were the kind of eyes it was best to run from, she thought, and yet she remained rooted to the ground upon which she stood.

"I apologize," he said with a smile far gentler than she would have believed him capable of based on those oddly charged eyes. "I didn't mean to startle you. I guess I didn't hear you calling out before. Lost in my own head, I suppose."

"*Nee* need for an apology," Rachel said quickly, happy to find the stranger such an agreeable man, and his tone so kind. "I shouldn't have been out here in the woods on my own."

"There's *nee* problem with you being out here," he assured her, taking a slow step closer, his eyes never leaving her face. "Sometimes, we just need some time to ourselves."

"Well, that's true," Rachel said with a shaky laugh.

"But, if you don't mind my saying so," he continued, stepping still closer. "You look like you're in distress. Is there something the matter? Something that I might perhaps be able to help you with?"

"That's really not necessary," Rachel said, her cheeks burning at how transparent she must seem to him. "I'm perfectly fine. I just got startled, that's all."

"Begging your pardon, but I'm not so sure about that," the man said, shrugging his shoulders apologetically as if he were embarrassed by his refusal to take her at her word. "Perhaps it will help if I introduce myself?"

"Perhaps," she said with a nervous laugh, hugging her arms tightly around her chest. "But help with what, I wonder?"

"I don't know," he said with a surprisingly warm chuckle. "Whatever it is that's troubling you. And, whether or not it will, my name is Samuel Weaver. And you're Rachel Fisher, aren't you?"

"*Jah,* that's right," Rachel said, taken aback by this new development. "But how did you know that? We've never met each other, have we?"

"*Nee,* we haven't," Samuel admitted, squirming with embarrassment. "But newcomers to Faith's Creek draw a lot of attention and curiosity, which I'm sure you understand. I've heard bits, and pieces of your tale is what I mean to say. I'm very sorry for the loss of your *daed,* by the way. I know how difficult that must have been."

Rachel nodded, then hung her head and said nothing. Of course, he had already heard of her troubles. It was likely that everyone in Faith's Creek was aware of some version of her life story. In a way, she was almost glad. It took away the pressure of having to divulge her sad history for herself.

"I hope I'm not making things worse," Samuel went on, frowning in such a way that Rachel couldn't remember just what about him had struck her as dangerous. "That's the last thing I wanted to do."

"*Nee,* you're not," she said quickly, some of the tension leaving her body in her desire to put her new companion at ease. "And *denke* for your condolences. It's very kind of you to say. I won't pretend that it hasn't been difficult to adjust to my new circumstances, although I've found everyone in Faith's Creek to be very kind."

"I'm glad to hear it," Samuel said, although he spoke slowly as if he were trying to decide whether or not to go on with what was on his mind. "But, if you don't mind my asking, why did you flee the gathering so quickly?"

"*Ach*," she replied with a sigh, realizing only then that she was hoping that he hadn't seen her hurried escape. "That. Well, if I'm honest, I wasn't having a good time. I don't mean to say that there was anything wrong with either the gathering or the people..."

"And I don't think that you are," Samuel assured her, holding out a placating hand. "It doesn't surprise me to hear that you didn't feel like being in a group of happy, jovial people. That's not really my idea of a good time, either."

Rachel glanced at him then, searching his face for some deeper meaning in his words. They had only been speaking for a short amount of time, but already she was intrigued enough to want to know more. She found no hint of what he was talking about in his eyes, however, and in fact, wondered if he'd forgotten her being there altogether.

"I'm sorry to hear it," she finally replied when she was sure he would explain his words no further. "But, I must confess that it feels good to have somebody understand me."

"I was just thinking the same thing," Samuel said with a grin, some of the momentary haunted look left his eyes. "And I was wondering if you might be interested in accompanying me on a walk."

Rachel's face flooded with heat, and she was sure that her fair skin was glowing bright red. For the first time since coming to Faith's Creek, however, the reaction was one of pleasure rather than embarrassment. She felt more comfortable with Samuel than she had with anyone outside of her *familye*, and she was just about to take him up on his invitation when she heard the distant sound of somebody calling her name.

"That sounds like my *ant*," she said reluctantly when the sound of Hanna's voice was loud enough that she could not ignore it. "I must have been gone for longer than I thought."

"And is it time for you to return home?" Samuel asked, real disappointment showing in his face.

"I think I had better," she answered with a sigh. "But I'm very glad to have met you, Samuel. Your company has made my heart lighter than it's been since I moved to Faith's Creek."

"*Denke*," he said with a rich chuckle, his cheeks flushing red. "I'm glad to hear that."

"And, if you should ever wish," she continued quickly, hardly able to believe what she was about to say. "It would be nice to have you come calling at the *haus*. I'm sure Hanna and Ephraim would be happy to have you."

"I might just do that," he said with a grin. "I think I really might."

Rachel returned his smile, and with a fluttering heart, hurried towards the sound of Hanna's voice.

CHAPTER THREE

*No temptation has overtaken you
except what is common to mankind.
And God is faithful;
he will not let you be tempted beyond what you
can bear.
But when you are tempted,
he will also provide a way out so that you can
endure it.
1 Corinthians 10:13*

Hanna was understandably curious at the absence and sudden reappearance of Rachel and asked questions that made that much clear. She asked her questions carefully, and never came right out and asked where Rachel had been, but her eyes sparkled with keen interest all the same.

Although Rachel was sorely tempted to tell her beloved *ant* all about her surprising encounter with Samuel, she kept it to herself. She had always been a quiet girl by nature, which had only increased after the death of her *daed*. For some reason, she couldn't quite bring herself to reveal her source of excitement.

Still, she struggled to sleep that night and found that every time she shut her eyes, she could see Samuel's bright blue ones gazing back at her. Her heart still beat as wildly as if he were standing right in front of her. It was almost as if his mysterious, lopsided grin had been imprinted there, and she now longed to have him by her side again.

She was almost as tempted upon rising the next day to tell Hanna about Samuel as she had been right after leaving the forest. For one thing, it would have been a way to explain the fatigue so evident on her face. For another, Rachel felt like she was practically bursting with the tale of their meeting.

As that day came to a close, and then the next, and the one after that, she found that she was glad she had kept her meeting with Samuel to herself. Hanna knowing about it, and about how hopeful she was about him coming to visit, would only have made his continued absence worse.

"How foolish I have been," she muttered to herself on the afternoon of the fourth day with still no visit. "How silly to have thought that he would actually come. He was only trying to be nice to a pitiful-looking stranger. I should have seen that from the start."

She was disappointed that Samuel had not paid her a visit, but she was troubled by more than just that fact. She was disappointed in herself for getting her hopes up, and she resolved not to make that same mistake again.

It was with this promise held firmly in her mind that she set out from the *haus* and headed towards the woods. All of a sudden, she couldn't stand the idea of being cooped up inside for one moment longer. She felt like she would crawl out of her skin if she spent another second looking out the window for a visitor that was never going to come.

In the woods, she felt the communion of trees, at least, and she took some comfort in that. She could get lost amongst those gentle giants, and a part of her was tempted to do just that. She wanted to just keep walking until she could make herself go no further.

It was stupid to feel sorry for herself like that, and she knew it. Self-pity had never done anyone any good as far as she had seen in her seventeen years. Admittedly, it wasn't very long compared to some, but the amount she had already suffered was more than some people lived through in their whole lives. Never once, had feeling bad for her lot in life, made a lick of difference.

She was ruminating on this while beginning to feel sorry for herself all the same when something made her stop and turn quickly. It wasn't a noise, or at least not one she could identify, but a sense that there was something there. It was like the feeling of a person's eyes on your face the split second before you turned to find him looking at you.

"*Ach,* Samuel!" she gasped, one hand moving to her throat while the other settled on top of her *kapp* to see that it was securely in place. "You startled me. I didn't realize you were there."

"I seem to have a nasty habit of doing that to you, don't I?" Samuel asked with a low, almost nervous chuckle as he moved out of the shadows and closer to where Rachel stood.

"I suppose you do," Rachel replied with a breathless giggle she could hardly identify as her own.

"Well, as sorry as I am, it seems like good luck that we've found each other again," Samuel said, dipping his head in a nod of appreciation. "Especially after I failed to come calling on you at your *ant's haus.*"

"*Ach,* that," Rachel said, doing her best to sound breezy and to laugh Samuel off so that he wouldn't see just how badly she had wanted to see him again. "It's understandable. I'm sure you've had plenty on your plate without adding a visit to a near-stranger to your list of things to do."

"I certainly didn't see it that way, but you're right," he said, shaking his head with what looked to her like real regret. "I've been busier than I would have liked.

It's part of why I've decided to take the afternoon and do some fishing."

"But that's work, too, isn't it?" Rachel asked with a suspicious frown that struck a chord in Samuel and made him let out a deep, hearty laugh.

"I suppose some people might see it that way," he answered, still grinning like a mischievous schoolboy. "But I find it soothing, myself. And, if it doesn't sound like too much of a chore, I'd be pleased to have you join me."

It was all Rachel could do to stop herself from jumping up and down like a giddy school girl. Here she'd been feeling sorry for herself that Samuel didn't wish to call on her, only to receive an invitation for an afternoon of diversion. She was starting to figure out that life had a funny way of turning things around when a person least expected it, and sometimes that worked out for the better.

"*Jah*," she said, swallowing hard to push down some of her eagerness. "That sounds lovely. I can't think of a way I would rather spend my afternoon."

CHAPTER FOUR

∽

*What, then, shall we say in response to these things?
If God is for us, who can be against us?*
Romans 8:31

∽

Once it was decided that Rachel would join Samuel on his fishing expedition, they wasted no time getting the adventure underway. Rachel thought about running back to the *haus* to let Hanna know of her plans. She worried that doing so would end the spell of

Samuel's being there, though, and so she resolved to go without making any stops beforehand.

They moved quietly at first, allowing the noise of the woods and animals to be the soundtrack of the day. She couldn't think of the right thing to say, and that was part of her silence, but it was far from all of it.

Something about heading to the nearby pond without needing a long, awkward conversation to get them to their destination appealed to her. Again, it struck her that she hadn't felt so at ease since before moving to Faith's Creek. Even with Hanna and Ephraim, whom she knew loved her dearly, she always worried that she was letting them down by being quiet.

With Samuel, though, it wasn't like that at all. They could walk alongside each other and simply appreciate the other's company. She thought this must be a rare thing, indeed, even when people had known each other for all of their lives. It made her wonder if *Gott* had put them in each other's paths for a reason, and if so, what that reason might be.

When they finally reached the pond's edge, some of Samuel's contemplative mood seemed to evaporate.

He appeared energized and invigorated by the presence of the water, and he laid out his fishing gear quickly. His attitude was that of an excited boy, and when he glanced in Rachel's direction, he had a wide grin on his face.

"Well, you certainly look happy," she said with a giggle, finding it all but impossible not to be caught up in his good cheer. "Much happier than I've seen you before. Although, admittedly, I've only encountered you once."

"I guess I am happier," he said, adjusting his hat on his head as he studied the placid surface of the pond. "I don't take much time to myself. I always promise myself that I will, but then I get caught up in the world."

"It's an easy thing to do," Rachel said softly, her eyes clouding over as her mind moved to the past. "The world has a way of consuming us if we let it. Sometimes it feels like it's just waiting to swallow us whole."

Samuel had nothing to say to this, and for the first time since setting out with him, Rachel felt self-conscious. She had never spoken of the more desolate, searching thoughts that sometimes plagued her, not with anyone. She felt terribly exposed now, and looked at Samuel reluctantly, afraid that he would think her odd.

If he was put off by her words, though, it didn't show on his face. Instead, he still wore the serene expression of a man entirely in his element. Looking at him now, Rachel wasn't sure she had ever felt that sure of herself in anything.

Still, without speaking, he ushered her down to the little bridge extending out onto the water, carrying with him all of the supplies they would need for their afternoon of fishing. He laid out a blanket and then took Rachel by the hand, helping her into a sitting position. If he noticed the way she blushed at his touch, he didn't let on.

"It's beautiful out here," she said after several more lazy moments of silence had passed. "I've been here for a little more than six months now, and I didn't know Faith's Creek had anything so pretty and peaceful."

"Really?" he asked, cocking his head to one side and turning his unnervingly pretty eyes on her. "It's

LOVE'S REDEMPTION

interesting to hear you say so. I guess people find beauty when they're in the right frame of mind to see it."

"What do you mean?" Rachel asked, shifting to face him more completely. Now, it was her turn to be made curious by a statement that sounded right, but that she didn't yet quite understand.

"Well, some people seem to find beauty in just about everything they look at," he explained with a slight frown of concentration. "And I've got a theory that it's because their hearts are full of joy. They see good things because they feel good. With others, though, it's not that easy. When your mind is troubled, and your heart is heavy, it's hard to see *Gott's* hand at work in the world."

"You're right," she said, slightly awe-struck by how perfectly he had just described her experience of the world since her *daed's* unexpected death. "You're exactly right. I've just never been able to articulate it so well."

"Would you tell me about it?" he asked suddenly, an expression of anxiety and interest lighting up his face. "About what happened before you came to

Faith's Creek? Only if you feel comfortable, of course. I would never want to presume..."

"*Nee,* I know you wouldn't," Rachel interrupted, feeling as though she knew him well enough to be sure of that fact despite not really knowing him at all. "And I don't think I would mind speaking about it. Perhaps it might even do me some good. I haven't really talked about it with anyone. I've kept everything locked away inside."

"So it must have been just you and your *daed* in Ohio," Samuel said by way of answer, gently guiding her further into the difficult and yet suddenly necessary conversation. "Or else you would still be there with your *mamm.*"

"*Jah,* that's right," Rachel agreed looking down at her hands, which were clasped so tightly in her lap that her knuckles were turning white. "She went to be with *Gott* when I was only ten-years-old. From that time on, it was just me and my *daed,* and we became very close. We built our own little world, him and me. I suppose part of me thought it would always be that way."

"I can only imagine what it must have been to lose him," Samuel said in a distant, somber tone.

"It might have been a little better if it hadn't been so sudden," she said, speaking more to herself now than to him. "If I'd had a little time to prepare for his absence. With him gone, though, I was adrift, and I've felt that way ever since. It's like there's *nee* place I really belong. Not truly. Even though Hanna and Ephraim have been so kind to me."

Samuel was quiet for a moment when she finished speaking, but she didn't get the impression he was put off by her revelations. On the contrary, his posture, and the set of his face, made her think that he was really considering her words. As difficult as they had been to say, it made her happy that she had spoken them at all.

"I'm *nee* expert," he said slowly, his brow still creased with that frown of concentration. "But I think sometimes people need more than kind words. Sometimes they need to feel like somebody is truly listening to them, truly seeing them. Does that make any sense?"

As Rachel stared into Samuel's face, she could hardly

breathe, let alone speak. She was so overcome by Samuel's understanding of her that it made her feel dizzy.

In that instant, nothing else seemed to matter, not his failure to come and see her, nor how out of place she had felt thus far in Faith's Creek. The only thing she wanted was to get to know this strange, handsome man better. She wanted to know what suffering he had endured to make him understand it in another so well.

She was just about to ask him for his history, and also for the real reason he hadn't come to visit her when a rustling sound in the trees behind them made them both turn. What Rachel saw made her mouth drop open in a perfect caricature of confusion.

It was Ephraim, storming towards them quickly as if he had a singular, time-sensitive purpose in mind that he intended to see through. He wore a scowl on his face unlike anything Rachel had ever seen, and he only had eyes for Samuel.

"Away from her!" he roared, his face turning a deeper shade of red with every second that passed. "Get away from my niece, right now!"

CHAPTER FIVE

*So we say with confidence,
"The Lord is my helper; I will not be afraid.
What can mere mortals do to me?"
Hebrews 13:6*

"Please, Ephraim, you mustn't speak to him so!" Rachel cried, scrambling to her feet quickly while her heart thundered in her chest. "He hasn't done anything wrong. He was very kind to allow me to join him on his fishing trip, in fact. He's only been trying to cheer me up!"

"You heard me," Ephraim snapped as if he hadn't heard Rachel speak at all. "You need to move away from Rachel, and you need to do it right now."

Rachel's head snapped back and forth wildly as she struggled to understand what was happening between the two men. There was something silent passing between them, something dark and angry, but try as she might, Rachel couldn't figure out what it was.

"I think there's been some mistake," she stammered, wanting to go to both men at the same time and therefore finding herself unable to move. "We weren't doing anything wrong, Ephraim. We were only talking and getting to know each other better."

"*Nee*, there's *nee* mistake," Ephraim said coldly, taking a menacing step towards Samuel. "I want you to find friends, Rachel, but Samuel is the last person in the world you want to get to know. Almost anyone in Faith's Creek would be a better choice."

Now it was Samuel's turn to scowl, and he got to his feet quickly, taking three ominous steps towards Ephraim before Rachel got her hands up to keep them both at bay.

"Do you think so little of her, then?" Samuel said hotly, stepping even closer so that his chest pushed against the tips of Rachel's trembling hands. "Do you think her so incapable of making decisions for herself? You should let her make her own decisions when it comes to making friends."

"I trust her just fine," Ephraim spat, reaching for her and pulling her behind him so that she could hardly see Samuel anymore. "It's you I don't trust, and she doesn't know enough about the people of Faith's Creek to know any better when it comes to you. She doesn't yet know that everything that comes out of your mouth might as well be a lie."

Rachel was so stunned to hear her normally mild-mannered uncle speak so harshly that she didn't fight him when he led her away. She only looked over her shoulder, sure that if her face displayed even half of the anguish she felt, then Samuel would know how sorry she was for the abrupt ending of their lovely afternoon.

Rachel stumbled almost as much as she walked on the hurried trip back home. Her eyes were too blurred with tears for her to be able to see straight. She had to rely on Ephraim to steer her in the right direction, and with him still muttering angrily about the sort of company Rachel had decided upon.

"What is this?" Hanna asked her voice tense, and her eyes full of worry as she met them on the back porch. "What's the matter?"

But Rachel couldn't answer. She was too overcome with the scene she had unknowingly become a part of. As she raced up the stairs, the only thing she could see was the image of Samuel standing by the pond, his entire body seething with anger as he watched her go. He had looked so hurt, so wounded, and it made her heart want to break to think that she was in any way the cause of those feelings.

"Please, Rachel, do be careful," Hanna called, close at Rachel's heels, from the sound of it. "You're going to fall and hurt yourself. You must slow down, all right? We'll go inside, all of us will sit down, and we'll figure out what all of the fuss is about. I'm sure there's a solution, whatever it is that has you so upset. Don't you think, Ephraim?"

Rachel's uncle answered in such hushed tones that Rachel couldn't make the words out. Hanna's question made her want to laugh, though, and to cry at the same time. After all, it was Ephraim that was the source of her current confusion and unhappiness. She thought it strange that Hanna couldn't see the guilt wrapped around her husband like a cloak.

"There now," Hanna said brightly as she settled Rachel onto the couch and sat across from her, although she couldn't quite hide the worry in her eyes. "It feels better already, doesn't it?"

"*Nee,*" Rachel insisted before she could stop herself. As soon as the word left her lips, she regretted it, though, when she saw the way Hanna and Ephraim winced. "I mean, *jah,* it's a little better. I'm just confused, that's all. I was finally making a friend, and Ephraim stormed in and pulled me away."

"She wasn't making friends with just anyone," Ephraim interjected, sitting down heavily beside Hanna and looking a good ten years older now that his angry indignation had left him. "She was with Samuel Weaver."

Rachel watched Hanna closely, curious despite herself as to what Hanna's reaction to the name would be. When she saw her *ant's* cheeks first drain of color and then flush with two bright spots of crimson, her feeling of disorientation only grew.

"What's so wrong about that?" she demanded when neither Hanna or Ephraim spoke further on the matter. "If there's a reason why I shouldn't spend time with him, I wish somebody would tell me what it is. It hardly seems fair, otherwise, and you're confusing me."

"You're right," Ephraim answered, his voice steady, although Rachel thought she sensed an air of remorse about him. "I know it must be difficult to understand, but Samuel isn't the sort you want to throw your lot in with. He's a bad apple, and as harsh as the sentiment sounds, it's applicable when it comes to him."

"But why?" Rachel asked, her need to understand bordering on stark desperation now.

"He's not from Faith's Creek originally," Hanna answered quietly, seeming to sense that Ephraim was at the end of what he could do with the situation. "His parents sent him here when he returned from his *Rumspringa*. It's said that he came home with a poor attitude, and they feared for what would become of him."

"All right," Rachel said hesitantly, doing her best to find some semblance of the person she had met in the man Hanna was describing to her now. "But surely people can change. Perhaps there was some reason nobody here knows, for him behaving that way."

"Except that the bad behavior didn't stop when he moved to Faith's Creek," Ephraim said with a conciliatory sigh. "He works at a nearby farm, and it's said that he consistently gives his employer, Matthew Schmucker, lip."

"And if that weren't bad enough," Hanna added, speaking quickly as if driven by adrenaline and a desire for the three of them to be on the same page. "He also has a reputation for getting into fights. He's the last boy in Faith's Creek that any respectable girl would choose to spend time with."

It would have been bad coming from Ephraim, but hearing such harsh words from mild-mannered Hanna was borderline devastating. There could be *nee* bravado in it, but only what she believed to be true, and Rachel thought that was the worst of all.

"Please, Rachel, promise me," Ephraim said suddenly, his eyes growing wild. "Promise me that you'll stay away from Samuel from now on. Nothing good will come of the two of you spending any more time together."

And before Rachel could think better of it, she found herself agreeing. Even so, she knew that it was a promise she might not be able to keep. As little as she knew Samuel, she was drawn to him, and she wasn't confident that a warning and a grudging promise would be enough to keep her away.

CHAPTER SIX

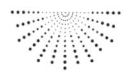

~

Whatever you have learned or received or heard from me, or seen in me—put it into practice. And the God of peace will be with you.
Philippians 4:9

~

As unsure as she was about being able to follow through on her promise to Hanna and Ephraim, Rachel resolved to do her best. It wasn't like she didn't have experience with isolating herself. It was exactly what she had been doing since arriving in Faith's Creek. It shouldn't be that hard for her to continue.

The problem was, she couldn't seem to make herself satisfied with being alone anymore. Before meeting Samuel, she had started to believe that she was *nee* longer fit for human companionship. She had started to think that she might just be broken. Now, she found that she craved her new friendship with such fervor that it was a physical pain.

Still, she remained close to the *haus,* determined to return Hanna and Ephraim's kindness by honoring their wishes. There was a part of her that knew she would not be able to stay away from Samuel for good, though, *nee* matter how good her intentions were. It felt as though his heart was calling out to her across the distance and the divide created by her *familye's* reservations.

So it was that when she finally left the confines of the *haus* after almost a week, she found herself wandering aimlessly in the woods. She felt as though she were looking for something, although she could not admit to herself what.

When she moved out of the trees and into a clearing

to find a *haus* standing there, she was hardly surprised. Part of her already knew that she would. That didn't stop her heart from leaping when she spotted Samuel toiling in the fields. It made her stomach churn, and she couldn't help remembering the look on his face as Ephraim had led her away.

Perhaps he wouldn't be pleased to see her? She wouldn't blame him if he judged her for being unable to stand up to Ephraim's tirade. He had gone out of his way to befriend her, to make her feel that she belonged in Faith's Creek, and she had failed to do the same for him when the time came.

Swallowing down her nerves and trying to drive the questions from her mind, she crept forward, her eyes locked on his working form. She knew that he might look up and see her at any second, and yet she couldn't make herself look away.

The things Ephraim and Hanna had told her about the young man did nothing to diminish her attraction to him. If anything, it was more pronounced now that she was seeing him putting his physicality to work. He looked unhappy, dreadfully unhappy, there was *nee* denying that, but he also looked perfectly in his element. He was so handsome that it was enough to take her breath away.

"*Ach!*" she gasped quietly, beginning to tremble all over when he looked up and saw her standing there. "I... I'm sorry, I didn't mean to."

"Didn't mean to what?" he asked, his expression unreadable as he sauntered towards her. "Didn't mean to stand there?"

"*Nee,*" she stammered, her face hot as her confusion grew. "I mean, *jah*, I suppose. I don't know what I'm doing. I didn't mean to come here. I didn't even know you lived in this direction."

"And why would you?" he asked with a chuckle, although there was a hard edge to it that made her stomach churn. "I'm sure that your *ant* and uncle didn't tell you. They wouldn't want you to think better of their warnings and search me out."

Rachel swallowed hard and lowered her eyes to the ground in embarrassment and shame. She wanted to be able to tell him that she hadn't heard anything at all, but she wasn't going to lie to him. She felt caught between two different worlds, both of which she wanted to be a part of.

"It's fine," he said dully when he realized she couldn't think of what to say. "I'm sure they've told you all of the terrible things about me."

"That's right," she said, suddenly emboldened when she saw how resigned he was to his fate. "They told me plenty. Now, I would like to hear it from you. Nobody knows what happened better than you do, after all. I would like to hear the truth."

He seemed surprised by this, and the way his eyebrows shot up and disappeared beneath the brim of his hat was almost comical enough to make Rachel laugh. She sensed that to do so would rob her of any chance she might have to understand the real Samuel, though, and she was grateful for the ability to maintain a passive expression.

"Are you sure?" he asked, the child-like uncertainty in his face enough to make Rachel's heart want to break.

"I'm sure," she said firmly, knowing without a shadow of a doubt that she wanted to be there for this man if she could. "And your employer is nearby, isn't he?"

"*Jah,* that's right," Samuel answered, giving her just a

ghost of a smile before returning to solemnity. "Why do you ask?"

"Because," she said decisively, hoping she looked just a little bit more confident than she felt. "We're going to find a nice place to sit, and you're going to tell me what really happened."

CHAPTER SEVEN

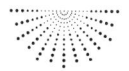

*Be on your guard;
stand firm in the faith;
be courageous; be strong.*
1 Corinthians 16:13

Rachel half expected Samuel to put up a fight. She wouldn't be surprised if he had a resurgence of anger and told her to get as far away from him as her legs could carry her. After the way she had behaved by the pond, she wouldn't blame him for giving her the cold shoulder.

If he was tempted to do so, though, the impulse didn't show on his face. He laid a hand on her shoulder, sending a shiver up her spine, before taking back the contact and nodding silently towards the nearby barn.

Taking her by the hand, he led her inside, and then up a sturdy ladder that led to the barn's loft. They moved to the very edge of the loft doors, which were open wide. Sitting on the very edge of the old, wooden planks and looking out at the land, Rachel felt like she had the whole world at her feet. It struck her how good *Gott* was despite all of the pain.

"It can seem so lonely sometimes, can't it?" Samuel said suddenly, his words in sharp contrast to her own rose-colored thoughts. "Trying to navigate this world."

"*Jah*, I suppose it can be," she said, laying a comforting hand on his, which was laying open on the planks beside her, and so close that she could practically feel his warmth.

"Until you're able to find somebody who understands you," he went on as if in a dream. "When that happens, everything starts to make a little more sense. You start to see that maybe *Gott* has a plan for you, after all."

What happened next was so quick that Rachel almost didn't have time to react. One minute Samuel was speaking in his soft, sad voice so that Rachel felt like he didn't remember who he was talking to.

The next, he leaned in, his face close enough to her that his enchanting eyes seemed to be the only thing that was real. He was going to kiss her, she realized with a start, and for a heart-stopping moment, she was sure that she was going to let him.

"*Nee,*" she gasped, wrenching her hand away from his and pushing him away at the last possible second. "Please, Samuel, you can't. You must know that."

"You're right," he said, shrinking back with a shocked expression on his face that made her sure he hadn't planned that move before he made it. "I'm sorry. I don't know what came over me. I'll go."

"*Nee,*" she laughed breathlessly, amazed by the way her body still tingled from that brief, almost kiss. "I don't want you to go. I meant it when I said that I wanted to hear from you about what happened. I've told you about my life, my past. I'd like it if you trusted me enough to do the same."

"You're right," he said with a sigh, shaking his head like he couldn't believe what he'd just tried to do. "Although in truth, I'm not sure what there is to say."

"The truth, Samuel," she said, both gentle and firm. "The only thing that's ever worth saying at all."

"You may be right, but it's not a nice story to hear," Samuel said, his voice becoming grim. "I grew up without a *mamm*. I never even met the woman who birthed me. My *daed*, although he might have been a decent man at one time, was far from that for as far back as I can remember."

"What did he do?" Rachel asked in a small, timid voice. All of a sudden, she worried that the source of his pain might be greater than even her own.

"He was an angry, bitter man, and it made him abusive. When he couldn't find an outlet for his feelings, he took it out on me. He hurt me to make himself feel better, and he didn't seem to find anything wrong with the arrangement."

This time, it was she who reached out, taking his

hand in lieu of words she did not have. He looked at her when their fingers met, and the naked gratitude she saw in his eyes was heart-stirring.

"I don't know why I returned home from my *Rumspringa*," he continued. "I really don't. I never wanted to give up the community, and I had *nee* desire to join the world of the *Englischer*, but it would have been better than going back to that man."

"Why did you, then?" Rachel asked, her eyes clouded with tears at the thought of Samuel as a lonely, hurt boy. "What made you go back to a *haus* where you experienced so much unhappiness?"

"I don't know," Samuel said with a sigh that sounded far too tired for a man as young as he. "I didn't fit in the world of the *Englischer*, either. It was so loud, so unhappy. I went home because I couldn't think of where else to go. I went with a new determination, though, not to allow my *daed* to push me around. I suppose that's why he sent me away. He was never a man who took well to being challenged."

"And the farm?" Rachel continued relentlessly. There was a part of her that thought she should stop pressing him, but she persisted nonetheless.

"What about it?" he asked, the edge in his voice only further provoking her desire for an answer to her question.

"Why do you stay here?" she pushed on, determined to understand everything now. "It's obvious to me that you don't like it. I could tell that right off, just by the expression on your face as you worked in the field. You don't seem to be content."

"You're right about that," Samuel agreed with a defensive shrug. "But what does that really matter in the end?"

"I should think it matters a great deal," Rachel answered, taken aback by the stark question. "Don't you want to be happy?"

"It's not a matter of whether or not I want it," he said quietly, once again staring forlornly out at a piece of beautiful land that did not belong to him. "It's just that I've started to think that there's *nee* place where I even halfway belong, and if a man can't belong to someplace or somebody, I don't believe happiness is part of the path he will walk."

"I know that feeling all too well," Rachel said, staring at Samuel openly now, like a moth drawn to a flame.

"I've felt it ever since my *daed* went to be with *Gott*. Maybe..."

"Maybe?" Samuel repeated when Rachel trailed off, unsure of whether or not she truly wanted to continue.

"Maybe we were meant to find each other," she whispered, losing herself in his beautiful, haunted eyes.

This time, when he took her hand, she made *nee* attempt to stop him, nor to pull away. All at once, it seemed that they had always been headed for this moment. As frightening as it was, she felt the truth of her words with her entire being.

"I must confess, I've dreamed as much, although I haven't allowed myself to hope that the dream might come to fruition," he said, his voice actually shaking as he clung to her hand tighter. "What I *do* know is that the dark waters of my soul seem to calm whenever you are near. I'm *nee* longer adrift, and I feel like I have a home of my own."

This time, it was Rachel who leaned in for a kiss, allowing their lips to brush so gently that it might not have happened at all. It wasn't that she didn't remember her uncle's warnings, or that she didn't care; it was that she understood now that they were misguided and ill-informed. Samuel was not the man Faith's Creek believed him to be, and she was the only one who understood that.

"*Nee!*" Came Ephraim's voice from behind them, standing in the opening where the ladder met the barn loft's floor. It was impossible that he was here, and yet it was a horribly, irrefutable truth. "I warned you. I warned you both!"

"But, Ephraim, please!" Rachel cried, sure that if she could only make Ephraim stop and listen to the truth, he could be made to see reason. "You don't understand!"

"*Ach,* I understand," he spat back, thundering towards them like a wild beast escaped from his cage. "I understand everything I need to know. But if my words aren't enough for you, Samuel Weaver, perhaps my hand can make you understand."

In the time it took Rachel to draw in a breath to protest, Ephraim was across the loft's floor, the planks groaning in protest of his sudden movements. Before she could say anything or do more than scramble to her feet, Ephraim had Samuel roughly by the arms.

"Stop it!" she screamed, her mind racing a hundred miles a minute while her body remained locked in stubborn paralysis. "This isn't our way. Somebody is going to get hurt!"

Those words would come to haunt her later when the whole awful scene came to its bitter end. She would close her eyes, see what happened, and feel as though her words alone had caused the disaster.

At the moment, however, it felt like everything was moving in slow motion. She could see every line of anger etched in Ephraim's face and the expression of bewilderment on Samuel's face.

Then, horrified, she saw his eyes widen as he took one step too many backward. His arms pinwheeled, and his entire body strained forward, struggling for a balance that would not come.

One moment, he was teetering on the edge of the loft, and she was sure that he would be okay. The next, he was gone, falling through the air, and the only thing Rachel could hear was the sound of her own scream.

CHAPTER EIGHT

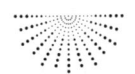

∽

*² Consider it pure joy, my brothers and sisters,
whenever you face trials of many kinds,
³ because you know that the testing of your
faith produces perseverance.
⁴ Let perseverance finish its work
so that you may be mature and complete,
not lacking anything.
James 1:2-4*

∽

The race down the loft's ladder and out to the earth in front of the barn felt like the longest handful of minutes in Rachel's young life. She felt as though she were moving in slow motion as if her legs had forgotten everything they had ever learned.

She was dimly aware of Ephraim scrambling behind her, that didn't seem to matter at all. The only important thing now was getting to Samuel's side, and hopefully, finding that he was alright.

"Please, *Gott*," she prayed silently, her teeth clamped together so tightly that her jaw was already beginning to ache. "Please, *ach*, please, let him be okay. I'll never ask you for another thing if Samuel can only be all right."

But the second that she saw him, she understood that he was not all right, although she couldn't know the extent of the damage. What she knew for sure was that his brilliant blue eyes were closed, and the face turned up to the heavens was ashen. He did not move, nor did he respond in any way to the sound of her frightened voice calling his name.

"Samuel, open your eyes, won't you?" she begged,

falling to her knees at his side and clinging to his arm with such force that it was likely to leave a bruise. "He didn't mean it, all right? If you only open your eyes, I'm sure he will tell you so."

"I'm sorry," Ephraim croaked from behind her, sounding like a ghost of the man he had been only moments before. "I don't know what happened. I never meant to hurt him; I only wanted to make him understand."

Rachel could hear the anguish in her uncle's voice, but now was not the time to comfort him. She thought that when things calmed down, Ephraim would recognize that fact as well. At the moment, the only thing that mattered was getting Samuel off of the hard ground and having somebody look him over to determine how serious the fall had actually been.

"What's happening here?" a man shouted from behind them. "What's the trouble?"

Rachel turned to look over her shoulder, hating to look away from Samuel for even that small amount of time, and saw the farm's owner, Matthew Schmucker, hurrying towards them. His face was contorted into an expression of concern, and Rachel could see that the man cared for Samuel, despite the boy's reputation for being difficult.

"He fell from the loft," Ephraim stammered, his face turning an alarming shade of red when he saw the way Rachel glared at him. "He was spending time with my niece despite me warning him to keep his distance. He wouldn't see reason, and I only wanted to show him that I meant business."

"You mean this is *your* doing?" Matthew asked incredulously, his entire face contracting with a frown. "You pushed him?"

"I didn't mean to," Ephraim said miserably, dropping his eyes in shame. "You have to believe me on that."

"It doesn't matter if you meant it or not," Matthew shot back, glowering at Ephraim as he knelt beside Samuel and gently slid his arms beneath the prone man's shoulders. "You wounded him all the same. I don't need anyone to tell me that this boy's rough around the edges, but that doesn't mean he deserves to be hurt."

"I know," Ephraim managed to croak out, his face losing its color just as quickly as it had come.

"Well, then help me get him inside and into his bed," Matthew said coldly, straining to lift the still unconscious Samuel to his feet. "I won't be able to get him there on my own, and it seems like the least you could do."

"I was only trying to look out for my niece," Ephraim said as he complied, some of the recent anger flaring up again in his eyes. "You can't fault a man for that, can you?"

Rachel stared at Ephraim's face as the words came out, and suddenly, it was more than she could take. She couldn't stand by and allow Ephraim to speak of Samuel like he was some kind of a criminal when she knew for certain that he was not.

"I didn't need protecting," she insisted, her words soft but grave so that it was impossible for the men to ignore her. "Whatever Samuel's past or reputation might be, he is still the first person I've felt a connection with since I lost my father."

Ephraim's mouth hung open, and his face darkened, but he kept quiet until they had safely deposited Samuel in his bed. With that done, Matthew went in search of somebody to fetch Doctor Yoder, while

Ephraim and Rachel walked slowly, as if in a daze, onto the front porch.

"I'm not insensitive to what you're saying, Rachel," Ephraim finally said after a period of silence that felt like it would go on forever. "But I loved your *daed*, and I know he would want something better for you than Samuel Weaver."

"Well, I knew him, too," Rachel countered, lifting her face defiantly. "And do you know what I think?"

"*Nee*," Ephraim said with a sigh and a faint, sad smile. "But I have a feeling you're going to tell me."

"I think that, above all else, my *daed* would want me to find somebody who took away my loneliness," she said, softening towards her uncle a little now. "That's what I think."

Ephraim looked at a loss for words, and that turned out to be a good thing. For, when the doctor had come and gone, after he had delivered his dire news, it was better for everyone that he had spoken *nee* more ill words about the man he had injured.

Samuel would wake up, and *Gott* be praised for that but that might be where the good news ended.

Yoder also informed them, his voice as calm as his eyes were grave, that there was a good chance that poor Samuel's legs would never be of much use to him again. The fall was such that Samuel might remain at least partially crippled for the rest of his days.

CHAPTER NINE

∼

Be strong and courageous.
Do not be afraid or terrified because of them,
for the L*ORD* *your God goes with you;*
he will never leave you nor forsake you."
Deuteronomy 31:6

∼

Whereas the image of Samuel's tumble from the loft doors already seemed blurred in Rachel's mind, she was sure she would remember the walk up the stairs to his room for the rest of her life. Her heartbeat was so wild that she feared for her health, and both the stairs and the hallway seemed to stretch and grow with every step she took.

Still, she was utterly determined to go to Samuel *nee* matter how nervous or frightened she felt. It was Ephraim who had wrestled Samuel from where he stood in the barn's loft, but Rachel felt just as responsible as if she had pushed him herself. The very least she could do was to be there for him now, even if part of her feared that he would send her away with anger.

"Samuel?" she called softly when she stood in front of his closed bedroom door. "It's Rachel. May I come in?"

She waited, her ear pressed against the door like a *kinner* waiting to be caught in a game of hide and seek. She held her breath as she waited for his answer, desperate to hear one word that might make her feel welcome. When she became sure that one was not forthcoming, she shut her eyes for a brief moment, nodded to herself, and eased the door open.

"I'm sorry, Samuel," she whispered, intent on letting him sleep if indeed he was. "I wasn't sure if it was okay with you for me to come in, but I couldn't stand the idea of you being alone in here any longer."

For a moment, his head remained turned towards the window, and she thought that he must be asleep, after all. Then he turned to look at her, moving so slowly that it felt like time was standing still. When she saw the look in his icy blue eyes, her heart jumped into her throat.

"You don't have to be here," he said, his eyes leaving her face and fixating on a point on the wall in front of his bed. "I wouldn't blame you for wanting to stay away."

"But why would I want to do that?" she asked, rushing forward and perching anxiously on the edge of the chair that sat beside his bed. "I would have come up sooner, had Doctor Yoder thought it was acceptable. I want to remain close by."

She looked at him imploringly, longing for some flicker of the feeling of closeness they had built up in the loft. She had to believe that it was still there, but if she was right, it was buried deep inside of him.

Even so, after a second of hesitation, she took his hand in hers. She clung to his fingers tightly, willing her body not to tremble so that she could project strength and somehow make him feel stronger as well.

It might not have been enough to accomplish that, but it did capture enough of his attention to draw his eyes back to her face. His face was pale and haunted, but she was glad to have him see her all the same.

"I may never walk again, Rachel," he said, his tone making Rachel think that he must be numb. "Did Yoder tell you that? I may never be whole again. What would you want to spend time with a man like that for?"

"He told me," Rachel said, her eyes never leaving his face as she spoke and her resolve to help care for him never wavering a bit. "But he doesn't know everything, does he? He can't tell us what will happen in the future. Only *Gott* knows a thing like that."

"But, Rachel..." he said with a sigh, shaking his head forlornly.

"*Nee,*" she interrupted, squeezing his hand again. "But nothing. I won't abandon you now. We'll continue to find comfort in one another, just as we've been learning to do already."

Surprisingly, there was no more argument on Samuel's part. When she finally left Matthew's *haus*, it was with the first real sense of purpose and place she'd had since losing her *daed* and coming to Faith's Creek.

She went straight home to Hanna and Ephraim, determined to make them understand what she already knew in her heart. She was meant to be by Samuel's side, and it took surprisingly few words to make Hanna see that.

It was a little more difficult to bring Ephraim over to Rachel's side, but with Hanna on her side, they managed to get the job done. Hanna's next step was to speak with Matthew, who was more than willing to consent to have Rachel stay on at his *haus* to help until the situation stabilized some.

That was how Rachel came to live under the same roof as Samuel without the two of them ever so much as discussing a courtship. She was dimly aware that she might be hurting her chances of something like that happening by making herself his nurse, but that was a chance she was willing to take.

At first, she was delighted to find that her worries were unfounded. It felt like she was more in her proper place now more than ever, and both Matthew and Samuel seemed grateful to have her there. Every time Samuel looked at her, his eyes were warmer than the last, and as she felt her love for him grow, she was sure that his feelings were doing the same.

Except that it didn't last. The changes came in tiny increments at first, so minute that she could almost pretend they weren't happening at all. Samuel smiled less, and his eyes looked more and more distracted when she or Matthew tried to speak with him.

More alarmingly, and yet harder to pin down, was a rising tension in the air. Although Rachel couldn't say why she often felt as though she were walking on eggshells. There was an anger building in Samuel, and *nee* amount of work and positivity on her part appeared to make a difference.

And still, she worked doggedly to help rehabilitate his physical person. She could not believe that Yoder was correct in believing that Samuel might not walk again. She believed wholly in *Gott's* restorative power; she knew in her heart that He would use it with Samuel. The only problem was, Samuel couldn't seem to find it within himself to believe it as well.

"Come now, Samuel," she said brightly, three weeks into their arrangement and well past the point where his optimism had begun to wear thin. "It's time."

"Time for what?" he asked sharply, sitting in the chair beside the window that had become like a new appendage. "I've got nothing to do. Perhaps that's the benefit of being a cripple. I've got *nee* work to do anymore. I've got nothing but time on my hands."

"*Ach,* but you have plenty of work," Rachel replied, keeping her voice light and happy despite the way his attitude made her heart sink. "We'll get you up and walking in *nee* time, I truly believe that, but it won't happen on its own. We've got to keep up with your therapy."

Samuel laughed when he heard that, but it wasn't a nice sound. It was full of contempt that made Rachel feel ashamed of herself, although there was no reason why she should.

This was the rough, angry version of himself that Samuel had presented to the rest of the world. This was why so many people in Faith's Creek wanted to keep their distance and were willing to all but write him off. Samuel seemed to want to hurt her, and it was proving to be an easy task.

"You don't get it yet, do you?" he asked, his voice positively dripping with condescension. "I don't need you here. I don't need your help."

"But, Samuel..." she said softly, most of the power gone from her voice now.

"But nothing," he interrupted with a violent shake of his head. "I never had any intention of you staying around and hovering this way. It's not what I wanted. I only wanted a few sweet moments before sending you on your way."

"I don't believe you," she whispered, the first, fat tears starting to slide down her face.

"But that's the thing," he returned, impervious to her pain. "I do. I mean every word. You've outstayed your welcome here, and your company is *nee* longer wanted."

She had begun backing up before he was done speaking, and now she hit the wall, startling her so badly that she almost lost her footing. She felt dizzy and sick as if she had stumbled into some other person's life.

She had never been so confused in her life, but there was one thing she knew for certain. She couldn't stay here listening to Samuel's hateful, cruel words, even if he didn't really mean them. If she remained, she would surely lose her mind.

She took the stairs recklessly, with little regard to where she put her feet and whether or not she might fall. She moved so quickly that when she reached the bottom, she ran straight into Matthew, who looked at her with shocked concern.

"What's the matter?" he asked with a frown, putting his hands on her shoulders to keep her steady. "What happened?"

"It's Samuel," she managed to get out despite how tight her throat felt. "He's finally made it through my wishful thinking. He doesn't want me here. I'm not helping him at all."

"*Nee,* Rachel, that's not right," Matthew insisted, speaking so earnestly that she couldn't help but look up into his face. "Even if he said it, he doesn't mean it. He's lashing out at you because you mean so much to him. It doesn't sound right, I know, but he's afraid of losing you if he lets you get too close."

"Really?" she asked with a mirthless laugh that quickly turned into a sob. "And how do you know as much?"

"Well, I'll confess that he never said as much," Matthew acknowledged, although he didn't seem dissuaded from his opinion. "But I can see it as plain as the nose on my face. From the moment he met you, his entire demeanor changed. The worst thing that could happen to him now is your abandonment. With that, he would truly be lost."

Rachel stood frozen, caught between Matthew's words and the pain still radiating through her from Samuel's mean-spirited words.

It would have been so much easier to take Samuel at face value and to return to Hanna's *haus* to lick her wounds. She wasn't the sort of girl to put herself out there for a person, and the idea of doing so again only to be rejected made her feel physically ill.

On the other hand, she couldn't deny that she had felt something special between her and Samuel from the very start. Now, it was more than that. She loved him, faults and all. Matthew was right. She could not abandon him when he needed her most. She would have to redouble her efforts so that he felt safe enough in her love to return it with his own.

She retraced her steps up the stairs slowly, steeling herself for whatever reaction Samuel might have to her return. She prayed for *Gott* to give her the strength necessary to remain by his side, and when she was through, she opened his door again.

"What are you doing here?" he demanded, his face growing red when he saw her. "What...?"

"I'm here because this is where I belong," she said decisively, daring him to argue with her newfound resolve. "And because I love you. There is *nee* accident in the world that will change that."

"But what if I never have the use of my legs again?"

he implored, his eyes wide and filling with tears. "What if this is all there is?"

"Then that will be *Gott's* wish," she said confidently, crossing the room and kneeling in front of him so that she could take him by the hands. "And we will face the world together."

CHAPTER TEN

∼

*but those who hope in the L*ORD
will renew their strength.
They will soar on wings like eagles;
they will run and not grow weary,
they will walk and not be faint.
Isaiah 40:31

∼

From that moment on, Samuel did not question Rachel's place by his side. She sensed the change in his heart immediately, and after several days, she was confident that it would remain that way. They were truly in this together, for better or for worse.

Even so, it was by no means an easy road the two of them had to walk. Samuel struggled both physically and mentally, always working towards a goal he was in no way confident he could meet.

Doctor Yoder continued to pay regular visits, offering encouraging words to Samuel, Rachel, and Matthew, too. He never once repeated his warning that Samuel might not walk again. Rachel would never be sure if it was because he no longer held that opinion, or if he was trying to spare Samuel further pain. Either way, she was grateful for his silence.

Bishop Amos Beiler often visited, as well, and each time he brought with him a carafe of his *wunderbaar kaffe* and one of Sarah's lovely cakes. He was like a light in all of their lives, and Rachel was sure that he was another of *Gott's* plans to restore Samuel to his former self.

It was during one of Amos' visits that Rachel happened upon a conversation that made her heart hurt and stopped her in her tracks. She was carrying a tray with refreshments for Amos and Samuel, and she set it gently on the ground by the bedroom door and waited.

"Why don't you tell me what's on your mind today, Samuel?" Amos asked in the same friendly, benevolent tone he used with everyone. "Something is troubling you. I can see it in your eyes."

"That's true, there is," Samuel said in the halting, hesitating way he had of speaking when he wasn't sure he wanted to reveal whatever he was about to say. "And truth be told, it weighs heavily on my heart."

"Would you like to know the best thing I've discovered for that particular ailment?" Amos asked in a way that elicited from Samuel a bark of laughter and made Rachel smile from her place in the hall.

"Something tells me that you're going to enlighten me whether I want you to or not," Samuel answered with a chuckle.

"Unburden yourself," Amos said, speaking with such confidence that his advice could not be denied. "Our problems rarely seem as bad when we share them as they do in our heads."

"It's just that... I can't stop thinking that this injury is a much-earned punishment," Samuel said slowly, talking as if a part of him would rather keep it to himself, after all. "I've behaved so badly. Maybe this is what I deserve."

"*Nee*, Samuel," Amos objected immediately, and with surprising force. "I don't believe that for a second. You've already done your penance, and then some. And you've spent enough time feeling guilty. To move forward, you've got to let that go. You won't ever walk again if you can't believe that you deserve to."

Rachel swallowed hard when she heard that and sent up a silent *denke* to *Gott* for bringing Amos to them with the exact words that Samuel needed to hear. She was still standing in the hall when Amos left Samuel's room, and when he saw her there, he smiled.

"What do you think?" she whispered, hoping against hope that Samuel wouldn't hear her there. "Will he come out on the other side?"

"I think he might just surprise us all," Amos answered, a twinkle in his eye as he walked away.

"And I think you should leave him tonight to give him the chance to do so."

Rachel decided to do just that, although it proved to be more difficult than she expected. After finally delivering Samuel his supper, Rachel retired to her room to pray and think on Amos' words.

There was something about the look on his face when he'd spoken that made Rachel feel like he knew something she didn't. She felt sure that if she followed his advice, something glorious would happen, something that would change all of their lives for the better.

After her prayers, she drifted off to sleep with that comforting thought still rolling around inside of her head. It helped her to sleep so soundly that she didn't even hear the strange sounds coming down the hall from Samuel's room.

She woke early the next morning, and as soon as she opened her eyes, she knew that she could stay away from Samuel no longer. For some reason, she felt sure that she didn't need to. She hurried down the hallway towards where Samuel must surely still be sleeping, her heart going a mile a minute, although she wasn't exactly sure why.

"*Ach,* Samuel!" she gasped when she opened the door and made herself understand what she was looking at. "It's a miracle! You've done it. You've worked so very hard, and you've done it!"

Samuel opened his arms wide, and she hurried into them, relishing in the feeling of his strong arms wrapped around her and his chin resting on the top of her head once again.

"*Jah,* a miracle," he said quietly, the feel of his breath on her skin making her shiver. "But one that would never have happened if it weren't for you. I'm standing now by the grace of *Gott's* will, but also because of the love of your amazing heart."

CHAPTER ELEVEN

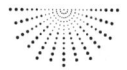

*The Lord is my shepherd,
I lack nothing.
Psalm 23:1*

Those first hesitant steps were the start of a new chapter for Samuel and Rachel. With Matthew by their side and offering constant encouragement, three steps turned into five, and those five turned into ten.

It was slow going, there was no denying that, but the

hard work was worth it. They had real hope now, and new evidence every day that Samuel was gaining strength. It was almost hard to believe that Samuel had ever given up on himself, now that he was so full of hope.

With each new small success, each tiny victory, Rachel and Samuel grew closer. Rachel had been fortunate enough to know the love of *familye* for all of her life, but she was still surprised by the depth of feeling she harbored for Samuel.

She could not imagine her life without him, to put it simply. She couldn't stand the thought of rising in the morning and not seeing his face. After everything they had been through together, it seemed to her that there could be no two people closer to each other in the world. She loved him, and although he had not spoken the word, she believed that he loved her, too.

Rachel found that she was perfectly happy existing in her little bubble of happiness and growth with Samuel, and she was sure she would have been happy continuing on that way for the foreseeable future. Even without speaking to him on the subject, she believed that Samuel felt the same way.

It was Sarah Beiler that first put into their heads the idea of venturing back into the world. She came to visit one sunny afternoon along with Amos, who continued to check up on Samuel's progress regularly. The two of them brought an air of possibility with them, and Rachel was more than happy to sit down to a cup of *kaffe* with the two of them and Samuel close by her side.

"I won't beat around the bush," Sarah said after several moments of happy but essentially trivial conversation. "I've come with Amos today with a specific thought in mind. One, I very much hope you will consider."

"All right," Rachel said uncertainly, glancing at Samuel for his reaction and receiving a shrug and a smile in return. "But, I must admit, you're making me just a bit nervous."

"She doesn't mean to," Amos said, putting a loving hand on top of his *fraa's*. "She's just excited."

"You'd better tell us, then," Samuel said with a chuckle that made Rachel wish that he would touch her hand the same way that Amos did Sarah.

"I think it might be a good time for the two of you to

attend another service together," Sarah said, her nerves at making the proposition showing clearly on her face and in the slight tremor of her words. "Now that Samuel is walking so well, and the two of you have grown so close, I think it might be nice for you to rejoin the community. I think you might find that they are more willing to embrace you than you think."

Rachel's immediate thought was to reject the idea completely, thinking about how unpleasant her first experience at a gathering had been. It wasn't that anyone had been cruel to her, exactly, but that she had felt like a stranger in a strange land. Now that she understood what it was to belong, she didn't want to go back.

When Samuel said that they would consider the idea, though, Rachel realized that perhaps they could not go on in their own little world, after all. People were not meant to exist in such isolation. That was a lesson she had learned all too well. And perhaps, *Gott* meant her and Samuel to find more companionship than what they had with each other. Maybe He wanted them to become a real part of Faith's Creek, as well.

They spent a week making their decision, and in the end, they were in agreement. They attended the next meeting together, hand in hand, and with their heads held up high. Rachel was surprised to find that she wasn't quite so nervous as she expected to be. When Samuel squeezed her hand, she was able to look into his eyes without fear.

"So?" he asked, the two of them hovering just on the outskirts of the service, which people were already coming together for. "What do you think? Are you still up for it?"

"I am," she said, smiling so big at the revelation that it made her face hurt. "I seem more at ease with joining the other members of Faith's Creek now that I have a true companion."

"I'm glad to hear that," he said softly, his eyes burning into hers and making her feel short of breath. "Because, I must confess, having the key to your heart has made me a different person. It's made me into a man that I believe is worthy of your affections. I only hope that you will continue to let me be that man for as long as *Gott* sees fit. I love you so much, will you marry me?"

Rachel couldn't speak. She was too full of joy to find the necessary words, but she nodded so enthusiastically that she almost knocked her *kapp* askew, and it proved to be enough of an answer for both of them.

CHAPTER TWELVE

~

*But seek first his kingdom and his righteousness,
and all these things will be given to you as well.
Matthew 6:33*

~

Six months later, Rachel could hardly recognize her life. Although there were many, reassuring parts of it that were the same, all of the comforts and community of Faith's Creek were still at her doorstep, the things that were different were all-encompassing.

"You are so lovely," Hanna said to her now, her eyes shining with tears as she patted down Rachel's dress for what had to be the twentieth time. "And you make such a darling bride. Not that I can really believe this is your wedding day, even now. What a *wunderbaar,* surprising turn of events *Gott* has bestowed upon us."

Rachel laughed and reached for Hanna's hand, the two of them sharing a moment of recognition of this most important of occasions. It was hard, not having either her *mamm* or her *daed* by her side as she became a *fraa,* but she was grateful to have both Hanna and Ephraim by her side.

And here Ephraim came, too, wringing his hands nervously and with downcast eyes. He looked like a little boy coming before his teacher to be chastised, and Rachel couldn't help an uneasy worry that he might be here to make one last argument against her marrying Ephraim.

"She's right," he said humbly, finally meeting Rachel's eyes, although she could see that it took a great effort and not a little courage as well. "You look very pretty, Rachel. I want to say *denke* for letting me be a part of this day."

"*Ach*," Rachel stammered, far more surprised by this than if he had ordered her to call the whole thing off. "That's so kind of you to say. But it's I who is grateful to you. To you and Hanna both. I don't know what I would have done if you hadn't taken me in."

"We were happy to do it," Ephraim insisted, surprising Rachel no end when his eyes filled with tears as well. "I have loved you like my own *dochder*. Which is why I must ask you for your forgiveness."

"My forgiveness?" she asked, more surprised than ever. "But for what?"

"For the way I dismissed Samuel," he said humbly. "I couldn't see him for the man he really is. I can see how perfect you are for each other now, and I'm glad that you didn't listen to me."

"*Jah*, so am I," Rachel giggled, going to Ephraim and flinging her arms around him in a hug. "But if it's forgiveness you want, know that you have it, and with my whole heart."

They left her alone then, telling her that they wanted to give her a few moments of solitude before her wedding. When she heard the door of the guestroom where she was getting ready open, she thought it must be Hanna come back with some last-minute piece of advice. When she glanced over her shoulder, however, she was surprised to find that it was another visitor entirely.

"Samuel," she said happily, turning to face him and grinning from ear to ear. "I was just coming to meet you."

Samuel smiled and strode towards her. There was almost no trace of his terrible accident left in his gait. There were other things about him that were different now, too, although none of the essential parts that made him the only man she would always love.

It was as if the weight of all of the baggage he'd been carrying around with him had been removed, allowing him to walk freely through the world. He had somebody who loved him unconditionally now, and the forgiveness of not only Ephraim but of the entire town for his previous antics.

As proof of this, if it were really needed, Matthew had given Samuel a little piece of land that he could call his very own. Samuel would no longer be a worker on another man's farm. He had a piece of property on which to grow his future, and it was where he and Rachel would build their future and their *familye*.

"I can't tell you how much I like the sound of that," he said now with a sigh, holding her close and kissing the top of her head. "I look forward to you being there to greet me for the rest of my days."

"Really?" she asked giddily, smiling up into his face and experiencing such a wave of love that it left her dizzy and weak in the knees. "Is that what you're looking forward to?"

"*Nee*, not just that," he said with a warm smile. "It's only one of the thousands of things that makes me so excited to become your husband. I already know that I will treasure every moment we have together."

"And when there is another little life in our *familye?*" she asked anxiously, as this was the first time she had spoken of the possibility of the two of them having a *boppli*. "Will you treasure those moments, too?"

"Of course," he answered automatically, although she couldn't miss the doubt in his face.

"What is it, Samuel?" she prodded gently, as she had been doing with him since the moment they first met. "There should be *nee* secrets between us before we are wed."

"It's just... what if I don't know how to be a *daed*?" he asked, hardly able to meet her eyes. "I didn't exactly have the best example, you know."

"But you did," Rachel insisted, clasping his hands tightly. "Just not in the man who raised you. But Matthew was as good as any *daed* could be, and you've had Amos and Ephraim as well. You've learned everything you needed to about love and the power of redemption it brings with it."

"I have," he agreed, kissing her forehead delicately. "But the most important lessons of all, I've learned from you."

Taking her hand, he led her from the room and out to the barn, where the whole district waited to celebrate their wedding. It was going to be a wonderful day.

15 TALES OF AMISH LOVE AND GRACE PREVIEW

Emma King hitched up faithful old Dusty to the buggy. The big, bay horse had been a present from her *Daed* when she first ventured out on her now flourishing baking business. With a sigh, she realized that it had been three years ago now. Three happy… but long years, three years where nothing had changed… Shaking away her sad thoughts, she hummed a hymn as she returned to the house and soon exited with a box of freshly baked fruit pies. There were all sorts, all homemade by her, and all her own special recipe. This batch included apple, strawberry, and wild berries. Her *Mamm*, Nancy King, followed closely behind with another box, this one of pecan pies. She had a light coat draped over her arm.

As they loaded the pies into the buggy, Emma felt her mind begin to wander. *What else can I do with my life?* Emma often asked herself this. *I could be baking for my husband and kinner,* she sighed. This thought frequently crossed her mind whenever she set about baking her pies—which was almost every day now. *I guess I have to resign myself to a life destined to be that of an old maid. Twenty-two and unmarried and not a prospect in sight,* she sighed again.

"Are you sure you want to deliver those pies now," her *Mamm* asked. "You've been up just about all night getting everything ready. That sigh you just let out sounds awfully tired to me."

Emma smiled her sweet smile. "*Denke.* But I'm all right. I'll hop in bed as soon as I return. It won't take me long, and the customers will be waiting." Emma hated to let anyone down.

Amber, Emma's younger sister, skipped out behind them with her satchel tucked under her arm. At eight years old, she looked so cute with her blonde hair tucked beneath her *kapp* and her blue eyes all bright and eager. Emma's two brothers, twelve-year-old John, and fifteen-year-old Joseph, had gotten up earlier with *Daed* and had already taken care of the morning chores. It was always a rush. Feeding and milking the cows, collecting the eggs from the hens, after that, they all enjoyed breakfast together, then the boys had left for school. Amber, as always, was pushing it to the last minute. Emma smiled, she was grateful to the two boys for their help in bringing in the milk, butter, and eggs for her, but she had a soft spot for Amber, and she indicated the buggy.

With a grin, Amber climbed on board, it would be much quicker if Emma dropped her off, and she knew her sister would always do it.

"It's overcast, so you may need your coat," *Mamm* said, as she placed the box next to the others in the buggy and popped the coat on top of it. Emma secured the boxes so they would not slide as she traveled over the gravel roads. She climbed up next to Amber, who was already licking on a candied apple.

"*Jah. Denke.* Bye, *Mamm*. I'll be gone all day as I have to stop into town to drop off ten of the pies at the Soup Shop. I may stop by and visit with Lydia for a short while. Do you need me to bring you anything back?"

"*Nee*. Nothing at all. Drive carefully. Amber, you be good in school and put that candied apple away until lunchtime," *Mamm* King said.

"I will, *Mamm*. Bye." Amber took a couple more licks before re-wrapping the apple in the wax paper.

Emma's dark brown hair was tucked neatly beneath her kapp, the tendrils that escaped offsetting her gray eyes. She was not what one would call beautiful, but she was fair to look upon. Emma had only one flaw— a flaw that in her mind was a major setback to her moving forward with the one thing that she thought was missing from her life... she was overweight, and no one wanted to court her.

"Emma, may I please spend the day with you and help you make your deliveries? You do look tired," Amber said. "I'm already ahead in school, so I won't miss much."

"Sorry, but you cannot miss school. Turn right, Dusty," Emma said, giving a slight tug to the reins. Emma made a few deliveries before dropping Amber off at the schoolhouse. John and Joseph were waiting for them. As she was pulling off, she heard someone yell, "Hey, fatso!" This comment was followed by laughter. Emma smiled for the sake of her siblings, but the comment cut her deep inside. Ignoring the hurt, she waved a cheerful goodbye to them. "Be good. I'll have a pie waiting for you when you come home. I love you."

She straightened her back, clicked at Dusty, and set out to finish her deliveries. After delivering her last ten pies to the Soup Shop in town, Emma sat at a small table by the window to sip on a bowl of potato soup, embellished with bacon, before heading home. She casually glanced around. There was an elderly couple having tea and cake. A mother and her two daughters were having a late lunch meal of sandwiches and soup. Two men were enjoying coffee. Everyone was with someone, everyone had a family... only Emma was all alone.

A nice-looking young man entered the shop, his eyes met hers as he randomly glanced over the room. He took a couple steps in her direction. Emma's heart started to flutter as she lowered her eyes to her bowl of soup. She felt disappointed when he walked passed her to the back of the shop. She left her half-eaten bowl of soup and hurried out of the Soup Shop. *I'm like a fly on the wall, no one ever notices me,* she thought as she climbed into her buggy and headed on home. *Gott, what is wrong with me! It seems everyone has someone they can share with except me. But who would want a twenty-two-year-old fatso?* Sadness crept over her and stayed with her all the way home.

She fought the temptation to drive straight past her best friend Lydia's house. It would be easier to just go home, but she had promised her she would stop by. Being a person of her word, she forced on her happy face as she knocked on Lydia's front door. Lydia had always been an encouragement to her even when she was not trying to be.

Soon she was drinking strong, black coffee with her friend as they nibbled on one of her special pies. This one was strawberry, and it was melt in the mouth delicious. Tasting of summer and all its promises.

"You deserve *Mamm* of the Year Award," Emma said to Lydia. "I just don't see how you can juggle a twenty-month-old, housework, do your gardening, and all expecting your second child any moment now, and still move with as much energy as you do. I guess some women just have a knack for motherhood."

"Are you saying you don't?" Lydia asked.

Emma shrugged, but said pleasantly, "I'm still unmarried. No beau in sight for miles to come."

"Just keep living your life the way *Gott* intended. The right *mann* will come along. He is out there, he just hasn't tasted one of your pies yet. When he does, he'll come running and panting after you and beg you to never leave him," Lydia said with a laugh.

Emma joined in the laughter, but she felt empty inside. Empty, and so alone.

"You seem to be taking it well, though," Lydia said.

If you only knew how much I am hurting on the inside, Emma thought. "*Jah*. What else can I do but to take it well?" Emma swallowed hard, knowing she was not being completely truthful.

"You know the Bible says to trust in *Gott* with all your heart and lean not unto your own understanding and He will direct your path and will grant you the desires of your heart. Good things come to those who wait," Lydia said. "Who says you have to be married by a certain age, anyway?"

"*Jah*. Who says?"

The friends enjoyed a slice of Emma's creamy strawberry pie as they conversed more.

A little girl clung onto Emma's legs as if she would never let go. In her throat, she was making small noises that were almost like crying, yet Lydia took no notice.

"Sandy seems a little whiny," Emma said, changing the subject as she stroked the child's head. "Do you want me to take her outside for a while?"

"Ignore her. She's been like that lately. *Grossmammi* says when they're that age, they tend to cling more to you when you're expecting another child. I guess she thinks I'm going to love her less," Lydia said with a laugh.

"Like I said, you deserve *Mamm* of the Year Award," Emma said. "I don't know if I could juggle that many hats at one time."

"Ach. *Gott* will give you the grace to handle anything," Lydia said.

Emma nodded, and they talked quietly for a while.

~

Instead of heading straight for home after her visit with Lydia, Emma decided to go by the creek. It was her favorite place for conversing with *Gott* whenever she was troubled. She had been stopping there a lot lately as no one seemed to understand what she was going through. Besides, she did not want to burden others with her worries. What good would it do? People had their own troubles to deal with, so Emma kept hers to herself.

Pulling Dusty up, she loosened his reins so that he could graze on the lush grass while she sat for a while. It was so nice by the creek at that time of the day, just before the children came out of school was the quietest time. The birds seem to be taking a rest from singing all day. Even the insects seem to be taking a break from hopping and flying and zinging about. 'Come, take a rest and lay your burdens by my bank,' the creek seemed to say, as it provided a quiet respite for all who would accept the invitation.

Gott will give you the grace to handle anything, kept running through her head.

"*Gott,*" she prayed. "It seems You made me different. I'm twenty-two and not married. All my friends are married and are living their lives. What am I doing with mine? Making pies. Is this what I have to resign myself to doing for the rest of my life? What's wrong with me? You made women to marry, to keep house, to bear children. I know I can be a good wife… so how come you have not given me a husband? Is there one out there for me?"

As she poured out her heart to God, the tears quietly trickled down, and she was lost in her thoughts and her sorrow.

A chuckle caused her to turn around. Some children were standing partially hidden behind the trees with mischievous grins on their faces. Emma had not heard them approach the creek.

"Hey, it's fatso!" one of them shouted. "Let's have some fun."

"You're as big as a house," someone said in a sing-song voice. "Where's the front door?"

"My brother says he would never marry you because you're too fat."

"Amber's sister is F-A-T. She needs to push away from the table more."

Emma turned away, but she could not stop the tears. Children could be so mean.

You can read these 15 delightful Amish romances for FREE with Kindle Unlimited Grab 15 Tales of Amish Love and Grace now

ALSO BY SARAH MILLER

All my books are FREE on Kindle Unlimited

If you love Amish Romance, the sweet, clean stories of Sarah Miller you can join me for the latest news on upcoming books http://eepurl.com/bdEdSn

These are some of my reader favorites:

A Spring Baby Dilemma

The Amish Healer Box Set

Find all Sarah's books on Amazon and click the yellow follow button

+ Follow

This book is dedicated to the wonderful Amish people and the faithful life that they live.

Go in peace my friends.

As an independent author, Sarah relies on your support. If you enjoyed this book, please leave a review on Amazon or Goodreads.

ABOUT THE AUTHOR

Sarah Miller was born in Pennsylvania and spent her childhood close to the Amish people. Weekends were spent doing chores; quilting or eventually babysitting in the community. She grew up to love their culture and the simple lifestyle and had many Amish friends. The one thing that you can guarantee when you are near the Amish, Sarah believes is that you will feel close to God.

Many years later she married Martin who is the love of her life and moved to England. There she started to write stories about the Amish. Recently after a lot of persuasion from her best friend she has decided to publish her stories. They draw on inspiration from her relationship with the Amish and with God and she hopes you enjoy reading them as much as she did writing them. Many of the stories are based on true events but names have been changed and even though they are authentic at times artistic license has been used.

Sarah likes her stories simple and to hold a message and they help bring her closer to her faith. She currently lives in Yorkshire, England with her husband Martin and seven very spoiled chickens.

She would love to meet you on facebook at https://www.facebook.com/SarahMillerBooks

Sarah hopes her stories will both entertain and inspire and she wishes that you go with God.

©Copyright 2020 Sarah Miller
All Rights Reserved

License Notes

This Book is licensed for personal enjoyment only. It may not be resold. Your continued respect for author's rights is appreciated.

This story is a work of fiction, any resemblance to people, living or dead, is purely coincidence. All places, names, events, businesses, etc. are used in a fictional manner. All characters are from the imagination of the author.

Made in the USA
Columbia, SC
03 October 2020